Rosy Cole's
Great American
Guilt Club

Books by Sheila Greenwald

Rosy Cole's Great American Guilt Club

Sheila Greenwald

The Atlantic Monthly Press
BOSTON   NEW YORK

FIRST EDITION

Library of Congress Cataloging in Publication Data

Greenwald, Sheila.
  Rosy Cole's great American guilt club.

  Summary: Convinced that she doesn't have any of the
things that matter, i.e. trendy clothes and a house in
the country, Rosy Cole decides to form a club which
will allow her rich friends to give her their surplus
clothes, sports gear, and jewelry.
  [1. Conduct of life — Fiction.   2. Schools — Fiction]
I. Title.
PZ7.G852Ro   1985   [Fic]   85-47876
ISBN 0-87113-044-0

BP

Published simultaneously in Canada

PRINTED IN THE UNITED STATES OF AMERICA

For Ursula Karelsen

Here's how it started. We were putting on our coats in the locker room on Friday afternoon the last week in November. Natalie Pringle said to Jenny Gilchrist, "Are you going to your country house this weekend?"

Jenny Gilchrist said, "Sure, are you going to yours?"

Natalie said, "Of course, it's snowing. The country is *soo* beautiful in the snow." Then she said to me, "Rosy, are you going to your country house this weekend?" and I said, "Yes, I wouldn't miss it for anything."

Chapter One

My name is Rosy Cole. I have a mother and a father, named Sue and Mike, two older sisters, called Anitra and Pippa, a cat named Pie, an Uncle Ralph, and an Aunt Teddy.

I do not have a country house.
I never did.

Back in the locker room, Hermione Wong poked me. "Where is your country house, Rose? You never told me you had one."

Hermione Wong and I live in the same building. We go to the same school. We're in the same class. We've been through a lot together. I am always straight with Hermione. "Do I have to tell you everything?" I said.

"What do you do at your country house?" Hermione asked suspiciously.

"We ice skate," I said.

"Oh, so do we." Natalie was amazed. "And we have this most wonderful pond and Daddy makes a little fire to warm our hands. The only thing that would be better would be to have our own mountain."

"We have our own mountain," I said. If I could make up a country house, I could make up a mountain. "We ski right down it."

4

"Lucky you, Rose." Jenny was wowed.

"Where is your mountain?" Hermione said. She can be relentless.

"Upstate." I waved vaguely out the window.

Jenny Gilchrist said, "Say, Rosy, could you come over to my place? I'd like to show you this really neat ski parka I got."

"Sure," I said.

I go to Read, which is a small private school for girls on the Upper East Side of Manhattan. At Read we wear uniforms to help us value human character over superficial material things and to choose our friends by their inner qualities.

Jenny Gilchrist never asked me to her house before. She must have suddenly noticed my inner qualities for the first time.

"I have to meet my mother at Bloomingdale's," Hermione sighed, as if she had been asked too. "She's going to buy me another pair of white corduroy Cippy Jeans and a Pineapple Label shirt in hot pink."

"I have three Pineapple Label shirts," Jenny smiled. "I'm collecting them. I couldn't live without my Cippy Jeans."

"Neither could I," I said.

If this was true, I hadn't been living. What I have is an imitation Pineapple shirt which is called an Apple shirt and two pairs of baggy jeans that were once Anitra's.

We waved good-bye to Hermione at the corner of Lex,

and headed west to Jenny's place.

The first thing I noticed was,
they didn't have any
mailboxes or directory
so you could see
who else lived in
the building.

The second thing I noticed was, they lived in the whole building.

Instead of a super on the first floor, the tenant was their car.

In the kitchen were the usual fridge
and sink and table and chairs and washer.
Also there were Mona and Desmond.

We weren't allowed in the living room,

or the dining room.

In Jenny's room she showed me her parka. It was lavender with pink stripes. Then she showed me her collection of Pineapples and her collection of Cippy Jeans and her jewelry.

"I just love my Delsa Repetti bean," she said. "It's only silver, but it's so cute."

I thought it was cute too, and while Jenny was in the bathroom it sort of fell into my book bag.

I was about to return it to Jenny's jewelry box, but she came out of the bathroom.

"Why do you keep staring at your book bag, Rosy?"

How could I say, "Because I just put your cute silver bean in it and I wish you'd go away so I can return it and not take it home with me like a thief."

"It's too full," I told her, and I meant it.

"My mother has the Delsa Repetti bean in gold." Jenny took my hand. "Would you like to see it?"

"It doesn't seem right." I pulled my hand away.

"She won't know."

"I have to go home now." I picked up my book bag and my jacket and made a rush for the door.

"Hey, wait a minute." Jenny reached for my arm. "You haven't even seen my

VCR and my video camera. I make my own films."

"You do?"

I looked around her room for a hidden camera. Had she been taking a movie of me stealing her bean? "I have to go home, Jenny." I yanked her hand off my arm, dashed out the door and down the steps.

Out on the street I was sure Desmond was following me. I began to run. I didn't stop until I got to my building.

As soon as I caught my breath, I called Mom at her office. "I have to have a pair of Cippy Jeans in white corduroy."

"We'll shop this weekend, Rose."

"I have to have them now."

"For heaven's sake, why?"

"You wouldn't understand." I began to cry. "It's the most important thing in my life."

"Rose, this is ridiculous. You aren't going anywhere."

"No, I never go anywhere. I just stay here all the time. We don't have a country house. We don't have a pond. I don't have a Pineapple shirt or Cippy Jeans, which even Hermione Wong has. We have a TV with no VCR and a kitchen with no maids and I'm ashamed to ask my friends over."

"Rose, really, what is the matter with you today? Are you running a temperature? I'm concerned."

I hung up.

If *she* was concerned, how did she think *I* felt?

And that was only the beginning.

Chapter Two

I went into my room and locked the door and dumped out my book bag on my bed. The little silver bean was very cute, but it made me sick to look at it. It reminded me that I didn't have anything and that I was possibly headed for the Juvenile House of Detention. I put the bean on my dresser and opened my closet.

Then I opened all my drawers.

Nothing.

I had absolutely nothing, except for a
Delsa Repetti bean that I had to get rid
of as soon as possible.

I heard the telephone ring. Anitra answered it. She was talking very quietly. I couldn't hear what she was saying over the police sirens in the street. Had they seen Jenny's film of me stealing the silver bean already? I would deny everything. I would tell them I had amnesia. I actually *didn't* remember how it had happened.

Anitra came into my room carrying two mugs of cocoa. She gave me a funny look. "Rosy, that was Mom. She asked me if I knew why you have to have a pair of white corduroy Cippy Jeans right away."

"Because everybody I know has them. Even Hermione Wong has them. Everybody I know has everything and I have absolutely nothing."

"Why are you pressed against the wall like that, Rosy?"

"Because it's fun."

Anitra looked around my room. "Where did you get the Delsa Repetti silver bean?"

"My friend Jenny said I could sort of borrow it."

Anitra gave me another funny look. "You seem upset, Rosy. Have a nice mug of cocoa and try to relax." She turned on the TV.

It seemed to me that everybody knew something.

"I can't take this," I said to my cocoa. I went to the phone and called Jenny. "The Delsa Repetti silver bean."

"What about it?"

"It fell in my book bag."

"That's okay, Rose. I'm getting the gold one for Christmas."

"I'll return it on Monday."

"Suit yourself."

If only I could.

The next day my mother said she would take me to Bloomingdale's. I called Hermione to tell her.

"What are you doing home?" Hermione said. "I thought you'd be at your country house, skiing down your mountain."

"We're going to shop this weekend," I said. "I have absolutely nothing."

At Bloomie's, in the Cippy Department, there was very loud rock music and pink and orange lights flashing. Mom said

the cut of Cippy Jeans was not for me. I said it was and I loved them and she didn't know how Cippy Jeans were supposed to look. They're supposed to be sort of baggy and oversized in places and tight in other places. That's what makes them Cippy's. She bought them for me. Finally I had my white corduroy Cippy Jeans.

As soon as I got home I went over to Hermione's to show her my new jeans.

She was wearing *her* Cippy Jeans with her orange Pineapple shirt. "I don't know, Rosy." She squinted at my pants. "Something isn't right."

And I knew what she meant. Without a Pineapple shirt, the Cippy Jeans looked awful.

I told my mother that I had to have a Pineapple shirt and not my dumb Apple shirt that's a cheap imitation.

Mom looked at Anitra. "It's like an illness," she said.

"Rosy, the Apple shirt is okay on you." Anitra was using her "poor you" tone. "The problem is that those Cippy Jeans don't fit."

"I love them," I said, but that wasn't true anymore. Suddenly I hated them.

I went to my room and closed my door. I still had absolutely nothing.

In my room, I took all my horrible things and put them in plastic bags. I put all the plastic bags in a shopping cart.

"What are you doing?" Mom asked.

"I'm going to sell my horrible things in the lobby so I can get money for a Pineapple shirt."

"Good grief," Mom said to Anitra. "Take her to Bloomie's and buy her a Pineapple shirt. Maybe that will be the end of it."

I felt better after I got my Pineapple
shirt in cherry red. I went to show Hermione. I noticed that she was wearing
Candy-Loo Aerobic Shoes in the same color
as her shirt. Next to Hermione, I still had
nothing.

That wasn't entirely true. When I went
to sleep, I had an awful nightmare.

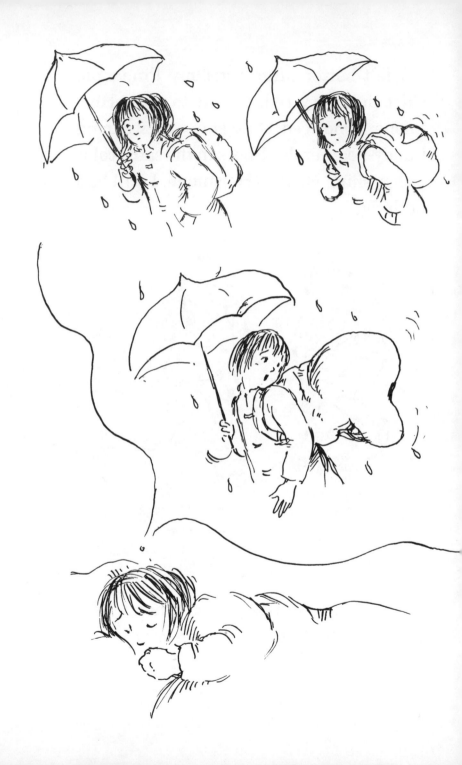

Chapter Three

Monday morning I couldn't wait to tell everybody about my Cippy Jeans and my Pineapple shirt.

Usually I walk to school with Hermione Wong and Christi McCurry since we live in the same building and are in the same class.

Christi is a model along with being in the sixth grade. When I told her I had Cippy Jeans, she said, "Cippy's are okay, but the new rage is Cuti-Club."

Hermione looked as if she was going to be sick. "I have three pairs of Cippy's," she said.

"You could wear them at home, or at Rosy's country house," Christi suggested.

When I got to school it was very hard to concentrate on what Miss Oliphant was saying about the topography of China. I kept thinking of how I could manage to get a pair of Cuti-Club Jeans.

Maybe for Christmas.

At lunch I gave Jenny her silver bean.

"I never would have noticed it was gone," she laughed.

"I never would have noticed I had it," I laughed back. "Only I opened my book bag so I could pack to go to my country house."

Natalie said, "It's a cute silver bean, but it doesn't compare to having your own mountain to ski down."

"No, it certainly doesn't," I agreed.

"We don't have our own mountain," Natalie said, "but I wondered if you'd care to visit our country house this weekend, Rose. We do have a ski club."

"I'll ask my mother." Then something occurred to me. "My ski things are up at my country house."

"That's okay," Natalie grinned. "You can borrow my sister's skis and boots."

All week I put together my wardrobe
for the visit to the Pringles' country house.

Pippa loaned me
her parka.

Anitra said
I could use
her waterproof
mittens and
her mohair
muffler.

Mom let me borrow
her new wool hat and
her old yellow goggles.
She said, "Rosy, you must
remember to tell the Pringles
that you've never skied before
and should go on the beginners' slope."

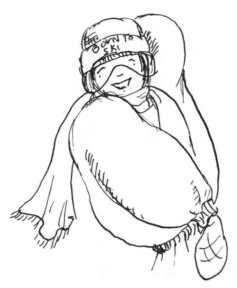

"Beginners' slope?" I began to hoot. "What can be hard about skiing? A chair takes you up and you ski right down."

"I'm trying to tell you there is a little more to it than goggles and mufflers and gloves."

"That's right," I agreed. "There's skis and ski boots and nobody in this family ever had them. Nobody in this family ever had anything."

"Oh please, not again." Mom put her hands over her ears.

The Pringles picked me up after school on Friday. There were Mr. and Mrs. Pringle and Natalie and Natalie's sister, Mary Victoria.

"Mary Victoria has outgrown her size-six boots," Mrs. Pringle said to me. "They should fit you nicely."

"Natalie tells us you have a mountain all your own," Mr. Pringle said. "I hope you don't find our trails too boring."

"The advanced trail isn't boring," Natalie said.

"No, I even got an advanced broken leg on it," Mr. Pringle joked, and we all laughed. I couldn't wait to call Hermione Sunday night, to tell her what a good time I'd had with the Pringles.

The next morning we got dressed right after breakfast. Natalie loved my Pineapple shirt and my Cippy Jeans.

"In the French Alps everybody is wearing these stretchy pants," she said.

"Yes." I shook my head. "It's the same in Switzerland. But I don't like the way they look."

We drove over to the ski club to put on our boots and skis. I'd never worn ski boots before. They felt like iron pots.

"The ones I have at home are different," I said. "They're French."

39

Natalie asked if I needed any help with my skis, and Mrs. Pringle said, "Maybe you ought to try the beginners' slope first, dear, till you get used to the boots and skis."

"Oh, no thanks."
I shook my head.
"I like a challenge.
It's more exciting!"

They adjusted
my gear and I
got on the
lift with
Natalie.

The wind was blowing, the sun was shining. Down below, little tiny figures seemed to fly over the snow. Sometimes they fell down for a minute. It looked like so much fun.

We got off the lift and Natalie waved good-bye. "I probably won't be able to keep up with you, Rosy, so I'd better get a head start. Wait for me at the bottom. Okay?"

"Okay." I waved and looked around.

I was on top of the world.

That was the trouble.

When I tried to move it was just like my nightmare. I couldn't.

I wanted to call Mom and ask her to
pick me up and take me home. I had lied
about stealing a silver bean and about my
country house and my pond and my
mountain and my skiing and this was
where it got me. Walking down
from the top of the world
in a pair of iron
pots.

My goggles were falling off. People kept whizzing by yelling at me, "What's the matter?"

One of the people was Natalie. "Rosy, what happened?"

"My goggles keep falling off."

"Take mine, I don't need them."

"These boots are too tight."

"I'm sorry."

"And the skis are too long and the poles are too short." I could hear my voice starting to crack, but I couldn't stop. "And the trail is too steep."

"It's too steep for me too," Natalie said.

"Only, I can't ski," I blubbered.

Natalie bent down and took off her skis. "Let's go over to the beginners' slope. I'll teach you what I know."

On the beginners' slope Natalie showed me how to use my knees and my poles.

"You're getting so good, Rosy, why don't you keep my sister's skis. Then you can practice on your own mountain."

"My own mountain?" The words didn't sound right because they weren't true. Telling Natalie the truth was working out. I kept going. "We don't have a mountain. I made it up along with a country house and knowing how to ski. I was jealous of you and Jenny having so much."

"But it isn't my fault that I have so much." Natalie looked upset.

"It isn't my fault that I have so little."

"It isn't fair, is it?" Natalie asked in a small, embarrassed voice.

"No, it isn't. I only have one Pineapple shirt and you have seven."

"I don't need seven, Rosy. Would you take one of them?"

"I'll think about it."

When we went back to the house for lunch I let her give me two Pineapple shirts.

"I'm sorry I lied about my country house and my mountain," I told the Pringles.

"It was very brave of you to try the advanced trail," Mr. Pringle congratulated me.

"The only trails I ever was on were in Central Park. My father used to take me sled riding. It wasn't a real sled, of course, just an old garbage pail lid."

"We have three sleds," Mrs. Pringle smiled. "It would make us very happy if you would take one, Rose."

"Oh yes." Natalie clapped her hands together. "And I wish you'd take my blue Cippy's too."

By Sunday I had made the Pringles happy lots of times. I was like their very own United Fund, Save the Children, and International Red Cross all rolled into one.

When I got home Sunday night, Eddie the doorman said, "Hey, Rose, somebody run you a benefit?"

"Could you keep this stuff in the mail room till tomorrow?" I asked him. I wasn't sure how to explain the Pringles' gifts to my parents.

Chapter Four

The next day, after school, Hermione helped me bring my things upstairs.

"What is this?" she asked me.

I told her about my weekend.

"I knew you didn't have a country house all along," she said. "You and I better stick together, Rosy. We aren't like Jenny and Natalie and that rich crowd."

"But they need us and we need them,"
I argued. "We should get together."

"You mean invite them to our apartments so they can wash dishes and make beds?"

"I'm not kidding, the Pringles loved having me. Just look at all the clothes they gave me. Some of them don't even fit me."

"Maybe they fit me." Before I knew it, Hermione was squeezing her head through the sleeve of Mrs. Pringle's pink angora pullover. "Oh, Rose, this is fantastic. You're right. We should get together. It's important for girls like Natalie and Jenny to feel they're being helpful. Also, they should know my head size."

"Maybe we need a club," I joked, "for people who feel they have too much."

"You mean a guilty club?"

"Yes, a guilty club." I thought about it for a minute. The words had a kind of ring. "The American Guilt Club."

"The *Great* American Guilt Club." Hermione liked things to be big. "For the kid who has everything."

"And her friends who don't."

I got the seltzer out of the fridge. "This is an idea that deserves a toast," I said.

"Also a campaign," Hermione reminded me. We clinked glasses.

It was time to get out the old oaktag.

The next morning we posted our signs on the bulletin board at school.

"What sort of help is on the way?" Mary Settleheim asked me at lunch.

"Watch the bulletin board. It will be announced," I whispered.

"How can you tell if you have the problem?" Betty Mazer wanted to know.

"Open your closets and drawers. Count up what you have and ask yourself how you feel."

After school, Mary called me. "I have four Pineapples and ten Cippy's and three Cuti-Clubs."

"One day it might hurt when you think that people you know very well have nothing," I advised her.

"What should I do, Rosy?"

"Keep watching the bulletin board."

The poster must have worked. My phone didn't stop ringing.

"I have everything I want," Christi McCurry told us on the way to school. "And I don't have any guilt."

"You are not being completely honest with yourself," I suggested.

Christi has always been a problem. She was probably still put out about my breaking up her club, the Christi-Belles.

"Do I have everything or nothing?"
Linda Dildine asked me.

"To be perfectly honest, even I feel guilty
when I look at you, Linda."

"Oh, thank you, Rose." She smiled in
her pathetic way.

"Help is coming," I reassured her.

By the time I posted a notice for our
first meeting, I was sure there would be
a good turnout.

The next couple of weeks were almost like the good old days before I realized I had nothing. It didn't even bother me when Mary Settleheim said her parents were taking her to Bermuda for Christmas, or when Suzi Milgrim said she had to go to Paris again and all they ever did there was "shop, shop, shop."

"What are you doing over Christmas, Rose?"

"I may go to New Jersey to visit my Aunt Sylvia."

"Poor you."

I was about to feel terrible when I remembered how guilty she'd be at the Guilt Club meeting.

After history that afternoon, Mrs. Oliphant asked to see me privately.

"Rosy, I understand you have organized something called the Great American Guilt Club."

"The first chapter of it anyway."

"And that the purpose of the club is to allow girls who have too much in the way of material things to give them to the girls who feel they don't."

"More or less," I said, not meaning to make a pun.

She looked upset. "You know, Rose, the philosophy of the Read School is to teach our students to value the inner qualities of a person and not the superficial and material ones."

"The philosophy doesn't work," I informed her. "Jenny Gilchrist never invited me to her house till I lied about having a place in the country. Some of us have everything and some of us have nothing and we all know it and it's about time we did something about it aside from pretending it isn't true."

"But Rose, you don't have nothing, and they don't have everything. Anyway, that isn't the point. The point is that you must learn to value yourself, not your things."

I realized at that moment that, though she knew a lot about the topography of China, Mrs. Oliphant was a very ignorant woman.

That night, as we were sitting down to dinner, the doorbell rang. It was Mrs. Pringle.

"Hello, dear," she said to Mom. "We've never met, but Rosy has told us so much about you. We wanted to do what we could to help."

"Help what?" Mom looked at me.

"A relief program we're organizing at school," I mumbled fast.

"Oh, Rosy can be so touchingly funny." Mrs. Pringle patted my head. "At any rate, there's a good selection of canned goods here and some more clothes for Rosy. They were Mary Victoria's, so they should fit."

"*More* clothes?" my mother repeated very slowly as if she didn't understand the words.

"I don't want to interrupt your dinner." Mrs. Pringle set the shopping bags down.

"I can't imagine what Rose has been telling you," Mom stammered, "but we certainly don't need secondhand clothes."

Mrs. Pringle smiled gently. "It isn't a sin to be poor. Remember, our charity helps us as much as it does you." She bowed her head and closed the door.

My mother leaned against the wall. She looked as if she might fall down. "Rosy," she finally said in a wobbly voice, "we aren't poor. We have to work hard for what we have, but we live very well."

"That's what you think."

"You have a nice home. A room of your own, for heaven's sake, plenty of food, good clothes, a private school." Now she was beginning to scream a little. I could see she was getting steamed up. "You have more than your father or I did when we were your age. You live better than ninety-nine percent of the entire world and you don't appreciate it."

"I've never been to Europe once," I said, "or Bermuda or even California. We don't have a country house." I began to blubber because this always got to me. "I don't have anything."

Mom turned away as if she didn't want to see my face. "How on earth did I raise such a selfish, spoiled brat?" she asked Anitra and Pippa and Dad. Without waiting for an answer, she stormed out of the room.

The next morning at breakfast, my father broke the bad news. "We are returning the Pringles' things," he said. "We have decided that to help you understand who you are, it would be best if you got no more allowance and no presents this Christmas. Also, we forbid you to hold meetings of the Guilt Club in this household."

"No presents? No allowance? No Guilt Club? Who I am? I don't understand."

He picked up his paper. "Take a long look at yourself, Rose, and you'll understand."

I went to my room and took a long look at myself. All I saw was a person named Rosamund Cole who had nothing. I didn't like her.

Chapter Five

The next day was the last day of school before vacation. Everybody was very excited. We were dismissed early. All along Madison Avenue the shops were displaying Christmas lights and wreaths. You could smell the freshly cut trees that leaned outside florists' windows waiting to be sold. The whole street looked like a magic place.

"You'll never guess what I'm getting you for Christmas," Hermione said to me.

"You'll never guess what I'm getting you." I didn't tell her I couldn't guess either.

"How can you buy gifts if you have no allowance, Rose?"

"Because I can."

"You have no money to buy anything."

"I don't have to buy anything. I don't have to have money."

"Listen, Rose." Hermione stopped in the middle of the street. "Unless you plan to steal or borrow, there is no way you can give anybody anything for Christmas."

"Listen, Hermione, just because my parents are cheap and you are stupid doesn't mean I have to steal or borrow to give you all the best presents I ever gave. *It's the spirit of the season,*" I hollered.

"Don't get so excited." Hermione started to walk again.

Excited? I was furious. "I have to work on my Christmas list." I ran ahead of her. At home I made my list.

Then I started to work.

After my gifts were ready,

I wrapped them up

and put them under the tree.

When my parents came home from work, they saw my packages. So did my sisters. Soon I noticed a little pile that hadn't been there before. Though I hadn't planned it that way, I realized guilt had triumphed again.

On Christmas Day, Uncle Ralph and Aunt Teddy came over.

"I wonder what to wear with this?" Aunt Teddy said, waving my ziti necklace.

"A can of tomato sauce." Uncle Ralph squinted through his viewfinder. "Hold that thing up, sweetie."

He's a photographer, and he wanted a picture of all of us with our gifts.

"I'll treasure my necklace always," Mom said.

"I love this tie rack." Dad gave me a kiss. My sisters thought I had a future in the jewelry business.

I was so happy. It was better than opening a pile of presents. At least it was better than opening *my* pile of presents.

Here's what I got for Christmas:

I was probably the only person in the world on Christmas night who still had absolutely nothing.

For the rest of the vacation, I went to my Aunt Sylvia's in New Jersey. Since it snowed a lot, we played Monopoly and sometimes slid downhill on my cousin Tom's old sled. I had a good time. I almost forgot about the Guilt Club.

But the night before school, I remembered that I didn't have any Cuti-Clubs or Candy-Loos. I remembered how the girls who had them always looked so happy, as if they lived in a special world.

I decided that I would hold my Guilt Club meeting whether it was forbidden or not. It was my only hope.

Chapter Six

The First Meeting of the First Chapter of the Great American Guilt Club was scheduled for the first Tuesday after vacation at four o'clock. I ran home from school to get ready.

At the bottom of the hamper I found my hand-me-down jeans and the old Apple shirt that I wouldn't wear on a bet. I put them on.

Then I set up the living room.

"Why are you draping rags over the furniture?" Pippa asked me.

"To create an atmosphere of poverty," I explained. "I'm holding a meeting of my Guilt Club."

"But Anitra and I wanted to jam in here."

"That's okay," I said. "We could set out a little cup for contributions."

Nearly everyone in my class came to the meeting. The girls who had gone south all had tans to feel guilty about.

"I'd give it to you if I could," Mary Settleheim told Hermione.

"I'd rather have one of your extra bikinis," Hermione said.

Before the meeting started, we got generic apple juice and Oreos and went to listen to my sisters jam.

"I love your house," Jenny said. "It's so cozy and warm. I love the way we're allowed in the living room and can even eat there."

"We're allowed to eat in the living room because the kitchen chairs are broken. I like your house better," I said. If she liked my place too much, she'd forget about being guilty. "It's time to call the meeting to order." We all squeezed into my bedroom.

"The purpose of this club is so those of you who have too much can get rid of your guilt by helping those of us who don't have anything." I held up two cardboard shoe boxes with slots in them. "I will pass around a pad and pencil. People who have nothing, write down your size and what you would like. People who have too much, write down what you want to get rid of and your size. Then we can match up. Any questions?"

Jenny raised her hand. "I would like your Apple shirt and your jeans, Rosy, even though they aren't my size. Can I have them anyway?"

Was she crazy? "You already have too much," I told her. "You don't want them."

"Oh yes I do," she insisted. "I love them."

"Me too," Mary Settleheim said. "Maybe you've got another pair."

"Apple shirts and jeans are all over," I said.

"But I like yours," Jenny sighed. "They're so comfortable-looking, like this house. I love the nice used look."

"You have seven Cuti-Clubs," I reminded her.

"I can't sit down in them."

"It doesn't matter. Cuti-Clubs are the rage."

"I'll trade you my Cuti-Clubs for your jeans."

"Trading is not Guilt Club policy. No more questions." I didn't like the way my meeting was going. "It's time to write down your sizes and what you want." I passed out the paper and pencils.

After everyone went home, Hermione and I opened the boxes.

"What do you call this?" Hermione snapped.

"I honestly don't know," I said.

Before I had a chance to count up all the papers I was getting, the doorbell started to ring. It was Jenny Gilchrist with seven Cuti-Clubs, ten Pineapples, two Candy-Loos, and one silver bean. In the next elevator was Mary Settleheim with Hunky-Dory boots, three Pineapples, and two Cuti-Clubs.

"Try mine on first," Mary said. "I think we're the same size."

While I put on her jeans, I noticed Hermione's eyes were beginning to cross.

"You are about to have more Cuti-Clubs than anybody," she informed me icily. "I hope that makes you very happy."

I realized something strange.
It wasn't just that
I couldn't sit down
in the Cuti-Clubs,

or that the Candy-Loos hurt my feet. I
realized that a mountain of Cuti-Clubs
and Candy-Loos definitely did not make
me happy.

It made me — Guilty.

Meanwhile, Jenny was standing in front of my mirror in my shirt and pants. "Oh, I love the way I look in these clothes," she giggled. "Like the way you looked when you were running the meeting, Rosy — all funky and free."

"I get to try them next," Mary said.

"Don't bother." I began to take off the Cuti-Clubs. "I like my own clothes."

"I really don't understand you at all, Rose," Jenny sulked.

I shook my head and looked around my room. I couldn't believe my eyes.

I had so much stuff. Why did I ever think I had nothing?

When Jenny and Mary and Hermione had gone, I went into the kitchen to put away the apple juice and the Oreos. My father had come home from work. "What's been going on here, Rosy?"

"The Last Meeting of the First Chapter of the Great American Guilt Club," I admitted.

"Why the last?" Daddy filled two glasses with leftover juice. "Did you just remember that it was forbidden?"

"No," I said. "Everything went wrong." I told him about the meeting. "I don't understand what happened," I said. "It's a mystery."

He put his glass down and reached over for my hand. "Maybe it's time you took another long look at yourself, Rosy."

I went to my room and took another long look at myself.

I saw Rosy Cole.

I liked her Apple shirt.

I liked her jeans.

I liked *her*.

That must have been what happened.